PETER HYLAND spen
in the Fire Brigade. Of th
all but three years were
rescue. Pete's work incluc
for airline cabin crew usin

and escape chutes. He was ....ng overseas students from Saudi Arabia, Kuwait, Bahrain and the CAR in the fighting and containment of oil fires and fires involving gas cylinders.

Later in his career as a station commander, Pete was invited to sit on an awards panel in which acts of bravery by civilians and service personnel were discussed and acted upon.

When Pete's mother died, he decided to maintain the family grave and surrounds as a mark of respect for her. It was on these visits that he noticed others gathered around the burial plots of their dearest. There was a common thread, in so much as they all used an old brown jug which lived close by to ferry water from a tap to their respective plots. When they spoke, sometimes in whispers, sometimes louder, it became apparent that they all had a tale to tell, and who better to tell these tales than the old brown jug. Thus, *The Secret Jug* was born.

To Dave

Happy reading from
the Author
Peter Hyland

The Secret Jug

Peter Hyland

SilverWood

Published in 2020 by SilverWood Books

SilverWood Books Ltd
14 Small Street, Bristol, BS1 1DE, United Kingdom
www.silverwoodbooks.co.uk

ISBN 978-1-78132-974-0 (paperback)
ISBN 978-1-80042-003-8 (ebook)

British Library Cataloguing in Publication Data
A CIP catalogue record for this book
is available from the British Library

Page design and typesetting by SilverWood Books

Acknowledgements

I only wrote the stories, that was the easy bit.

Thanks to Sheila who turned writing to typing, to Lynda the reader and adviser, Garry and his computer knowledge, and Enya, Viki, Catherine, Helen and all the team at SilverWood Books for their tireless work ethic and friendly approach. Finally, thanks to all you good people who bought the book and made it all worth while.

VOLUME I

Introduction

I never knew John Chmara nor his wife or children, and yet these past fifteen years or so I have never been more than a few feet from him.

I live in what I think is the Catholic section of a sprawling graveyard that covers many acres of land and is now full. Further purchases of land will always be necessary. To the east lies the city which it constantly serves. The site has a generous helping of trees and is interspersed with interconnecting routes. There is a narrow path close by on which vehicles are allowed, but with hardly sufficient room to pass unless one of them drives onto the manicured grass. There is a large bin with an up-and-over top in which visitors put their dead flowers, plants and grass cuttings.

A new water tap has been installed in the last year to replace the old spring-loaded time-operated device which constantly ran on.

Very few people know of my existence as I am partially hidden by a slab of granite which sits at right angles to the main stone. Proof of my concealment is borne out by the two milk bottles that lie at the base of the tap feeder-pipe along with other makeshift receptacles used to convey the water.

Ten people have used my services over the years, and these have dwindled down to three. It is these three who, over the years, I have come to know intimately and it is their stories I am about to tell.

Religiously they arrive at the graves, pick me up from my nook, take me to the tap, and fill me with water, then on to their respective plots where I replenish the flower vases with fresh water. As I sit at their gravesides I have listened while they have talked to friends, to themselves or even to the people interred. Sometimes they even speak to me. And then, as if on autopilot and with due reverence, I am returned to the resting place of John Chmara. I am *the Secret Jug.*

Think Bike

Chapter One

Molly Greer had not spoken for a full five minutes, she couldn't. She was so full of emotion. The tears rolled down her face as she stared down at the grave of her only son, Martin. The cutting wind howled through the graveyard as she grasped hold of her friend Sandra. The cold seemed to have no effect on Molly because she was numbed by tragedy. Slowly she composed herself and the events of the last four weeks came stuttering out.

Jim, her husband, was not with her. Since the identification of his son at the local mortuary he had become devoid of any energy or rational thought. There were no obvious wounds on Martin, only a depression in the top of his skull. It would be weeks before Jim would visit the grave. Molly understood her husband's plight and bore him no malice.

"We should never have agreed to loan him the money," blurted Molly to a trembling Sandra, "but he kept going on and on, telling us how safe he was and that he wouldn't do anything stupid, that he was ready to ride the big bike.

"We must have been bloody mad to have agreed to it," Molly lamented, her eyes red with tears.

She then stiffened and softened as she recalled Martin's lovely smile as he came home with his super machine.

"It was a year old, he had traded in his old bike and put most of his savings into the purchase and the mammoth insurance. It was our £400 that had clinched the deal. I must admit he did look grand," she half-choked, "in his black leathers and helmet contrasting with the flame red of his new charger."

As if a switch had been thrown, Molly returned to her world of despair. "It was Saturday morning, he had had 'Thor' a month without mishap. We sat down for breakfast when he suddenly announced he was going for a spin. 'Do you want to come, Mum?' he said, half-laughing. He knew what my response would be, so he was not surprised when I declined with an unspoken half-look. Jim refused also as he had been frightened of bikes since coming off one years ago when riding pillion and the footrest hit the tarmac when negotiating a bend. Says he can still feel the pain in his palms even now as the gravel stripped off the skin."

Molly and Sandra stared transfixed at the grave for some time before Sandra put me quietly down on the dry grass.

"Well, what did happen?" asked Sandra. It was her only contribution to the conversation that morning. Molly was visibly trying to compose herself, she looked into the far distance, unconsciously wringing her hands, and then, with what seemed as though an age had passed, she began to speak.

"Martin finished breakfast, donned his leathers, gave me a hug and waved goodbye to the pair of us. 'I'll be home about four,' he exclaimed. 'Be careful,' we said in tandem.

"We know he went to the local petrol station for fuel by the receipt in his wallet and then up the A46 Fosse Way to Newark and then left Nottinghamshire on the A17 towards Sleaford. He was snapped by a speed camera around 11.30am near RAF Cranwell. The ticket and photographic evidence came through the post ten days after his death. He was travelling 10 mph over the prescribed speed limit. It all gets a bit hazy then," said Molly, stifling a sob.

"He'd headed for the Lincolnshire Fens. He loved it there; he went fishing a lot with Jim and had dreams of catching a 20lb pike. Never happened, of course. It was always the others who caught the big ones," she reflected.

"The police car arrived at 2.30pm. I saw the officer slowly walk up the drive, check the house number and knock on the door. As soon as he took off his cap I knew Martin was dead." There was a long pause, followed by an agonizing groan, and then Molly continued. "A phone call had been received from a Mr Simon Long from a public phone box near the village of Stickney, a few miles north of Boston on the A16. Mr Long said he was driving his car when in his rear-view mirror he saw a motorbike come round the bend, clip the kerb and disappear into the bushes and trees at the roadside.

"He knew it was bad, but was too frightened to return to the scene of the accident. He pinpointed the location, close to a road sign and then hung up."

"I'm all in," said Molly to her friend. "Can we go?" Sandra returned me dutifully to my resting place, and gently shepherded Molly away from the grave.

"They never traced Mr Long," said Molly meekly as they left.

Chapter Two

Jamie Short met his old schoolfriend Martin purely by accident at the Esso station in Nottingham that fateful Saturday morning. Jamie's girlfriend was at work all day on overtime, and he was at a loose end. He looked enviously at Martin's new bike and felt a little embarrassed when he mentally compared it with his own. "Bloody hell Martin, it's the dog's," Jamie exclaimed, as his eyes feasted on Martin's bike. They talked briefly and then Martin said he was going to Skegness for some fish and chips, and that Jamie was welcome to come. Going to Skegness for the day on a whim was an old tradition for Midlanders and this was still alive in the biking fraternity. It was a must-do.

There was some banter about Jamie's keeping up with Martin so they agreed to meet at a transport cafe just north of Boston, for tea and a chat. Martin was on his second bacon roll, Jamie recalled, when he parked his machine next to a broken-down truck and entered the cafe. The conversation quickly changed from the past to the present and that was the bike.

Martin was crestfallen for the first few minutes explaining that he was sure he had activated a fixed speed camera on the A17, saying that the light flash was unmistakable and then bemoaning the fine that would eventually arrive, and the insurance hike, which he found already financially crippling. He had only blipped the throttle to pass a lumbering lorry.

Jamie had quizzed Martin about the bike's tech spec, as he drooled over the figures he was already subconsciously plotting to ride the bike. He pumped Martin for information; the answers gushed forth without hesitation, two-seater, chain-driven, big fat road-hugging tyres, he extolled its virtues! Slick faring, electronic ignition and state-of-the-art immobilizer system to ward off joyriders. The *coup de grâce* was its power. The top speed was the same as its brake horsepower. A staggering, mouth-watering 175. Coupled with the outstanding 0–60 acceleration times of sub three seconds, this was a true two-wheeled equivalent of a Ferrari motor car!

It took a full fifteen minutes for Jamie to convince Martin that he was fit to ride it. Realizing Jamie's insurance did not cover the bike, Martin had reluctantly agreed to the venture. The ground rules were simple: they would leave the cafe with Martin as pillion, travel two miles up the road to the roundabout, then return to the cafe, strictly adhering to the clearway limit.

The first stage was uneventful. They mounted the bike which was standing in a desolate part of the car park, obscured by a privet hedge and took off.

Statistics were one thing but actually experiencing the physical aspects of the real thing hit Jamie like a sledgehammer. He was out of his depth. He knew it, but there was no going back. He was 'testosterone man'.

Returning from the traffic island, both of them laughing like a couple of schoolboys, Jamie shouted above the wind, "Can I put the hammer down on Thor for a couple of seconds?" Martin glanced down the road, saw that it was straight for half a mile in front of them but with a bend looming in the distance. There was only one car on the road a hundred yards ahead when Martin uttered his last simple command, "Two seconds". Jamie twisted the loud grip a full half-turn and the front wheel lurched momentarily and they were gone, passing the gaping couple in the car within a second. He glanced at the speedo as the bend loomed, 120 said the needle as they approached the bend, his hand reversing the motion on the accelerator. The squirrel was not "thinking bike" when he attempted to cross the road, he had made the crossing many times before without mishap and only heard the throbbing exhaust of the bike as he became another piece of roadkill.

Jamie had tried hard, so bloody hard, to miss the hopping squirrel. It would have been a funny conversation piece later if he had missed it, but he hadn't and the kerb was beckoning. They were doing about 60 mph when they bounced off the kerb, catapulted across the road and hit the protruding tree stump with the front wheel of the bike. Both riders, driven by inertia, hurtled forward, the bike looping the loop, landed in a bush and disappeared. Martin would have flown the further had he not collided with the English oak head-on. Jamie was luckier, the handlebars of the bike were torn from his grasp as he cartwheeled through the air, missing the tree by inches as he crashed through the top of a bush, coming to rest in a slimy bog. He was completely unscathed, except for a minor tear in his leggings near his right knee. No one on the planet had witnessed the accident. Physically OK but mentally in complete turmoil, he walked the few yards to the oak. It was obvious no doctor was needed. Martin was as dead as the squirrel.

He sobbed uncontrollably for a time, returned to the bog, and wiped himself down with leaves soaked in the streamlet that fed it. He heard traffic passing but realized the drivers were unaware of the grim secret only a few yards away. He made a conscious decision to leave the scene.

He kept to the fields until he reached the village. It was raining as he entered the phone box and called the police. It was at that moment he hatched his plan. His friend was dead, it was his fault, but he couldn't take the rap. He had convinced himself that there was no point in owning up to the accident and that he would have to live with the consequences. He put down the phone, and like a fugitive from justice, headed back into the fields and returned to the cafe.

The journey of close to a mile and a half took what seemed an age. Trembling he mounted his bike, left the cafe and headed home. Only a hovering kestrel had witnessed his journey.

And so, it was that Jamie Short was at the graveside of his friend, recounting the story to the polished granite surmounting the remains of Martin Greer, schoolfriend, good mate and deceased.

It was not the first time he had visited, but it was the last. A couple of times before he had been to the cemetery and had noticed the car of Molly Greer and had done an immediate about-turn. Soon he had recognized her regimented visiting times and fitted himself in. At the funeral he could not bring himself to look Molly in the face but mumbled to her incoherently and left.

Jamie stood at the graveside for a full thirty minutes transfixed by the inscription on the slab:

MARTIN GREER OUR SON DIED ALONE
FOREVER IN OUR THOUGHTS

He then began to speak in soft tones addressing himself to his old dead friend. He spoke of the possibility of promotion, the chance of a new flat in a quiet suburban area, engagement to his girlfriend, maybe even marriage. There was a chance of a holiday abroad in the sunshine. All seemed on the up and up.

A week after the funeral his old friends had agreed to re-enact the run to Skegness as a mark of respect to Martin. The rendezvous point was the famous clock tower and he had agreed to tag along. They had sunk a couple of pints of warm beer and then proceeded to the chippy. All agreed that this was Martin's intended destination. He recalled that he felt they were all talking about him. "It was impossible," he anguished, but he couldn't shake off the feeling.

There was a long pause before he spoke again; it was as though some unfathomable communication was happening between the living and the dead. "What would you have done, Martin?" he blurted, demanding an answer. "Honestly now," he followed, softer in tone.

Bolt upright, Jamie stared forward, his mind trying to reconcile the awful truth of his actions. And then, as if on auto-pilot, he lowered the trunk of his body and lent forward, kissing the unfeeling polished stone both long and tenderly. Turning his aching body he left the graveside, his mind tortured and confused.

Jamie Short alias Simon Long was about to take his last ride on his motorbike.

Italian Beauty

Chapter One

The yaffle, or green woodpecker as it is commonly known, was a regular visitor to the graveyard.

He was desperately hungry following a severe winter. His main food supply, the common meadow ant, was hard to get at as the anthills were frozen or buried deep in the snow. It was a high price to pay for his conservative tastes.

But now it was spring, he had survived, and was looking for a mate. Although he didn't drum like his cousin, the great spotted woodpecker, he was revered by all who walked the avenues of the cemetery. I was always bewildered by the treatment bestowed upon him. It was like he was a mythical figure or ancient deity. "Look, a woodpecker," was the common exclamation. "Did you see that bird, it was a woodpecker," was another.

However, the stunted flight and the yaffle call of the mystical bird were lost on Maureen Sledge and her sister Pamela as they trudged to the grave of Maureen's husband John.

It was just over a month since he had died and the burial was about a week later. The harsh weather had claimed more than a few that year.

There was only a year separating the two sisters and they were good friends, which was as well, as they both wore almost identical clothes. Black coats buttoned to the neck, dark trousers and shoes and matching woollen hats. From a distance the only distinguishing feature was that Maureen sported a red neck scarf while Pamela's was yellow. How odd, I remember thinking.

Without speaking the pair began to remove the tired flowers from around the grave and place them in the large green up-and-over bin close by. They were replaced by fresh flowers that they had brought with them, and then followed a general tidy-up of the surrounding proximate area. Maureen spotted me and it was then my turn to get involved.

Pam broke the silence first. "It would have been fifteen years of marriage this month," she said without feeling. Maureen didn't respond immediately and then, following a slight quivering of the upper lip she began an unfaltering recital of her life with John.

They had met at an evening class in which Italian was taught. John was already reasonably fluent in French and Spanish and was also studying Portuguese. She was having difficulty learning the Italian language and in the course of time he was giving her extracurricular help which resulted in weekend visits to her flat. Romance quickly blossomed and the pair were often seen out together.

Holidays were always taken in Europe where they could exercise their language skills but she was still confined to smatterings of Italian, whereas John could converse comfortably anywhere in central Europe.

A couple of years after they met John proposed marriage and she accepted without hesitation. The honeymoon was to be in Monaco, a brief five-day whirlwind. Two nights were spent in the Hotel de Londres, a magnificent hotel, just a stone's throw from the famous casino in which they lost £50 in a few minutes. The motor racing Grand Prix was only two weeks away. They both walked the course down to the harbour where the splendid yachts of the rich and famous were moored.

A small army of workmen were busy erecting the crash barriers which had to be placed at strategic points around the course to protect the thousands of fans who would come to see the race. A number of temporary structures had to be removed prior to the event with meticulous care, and then replaced after the race. It was a mammoth undertaking which took place every year. How did they possibly manage to overtake on such a narrow, winding road, she remembered thinking.

The remainder of the honeymoon was spent across the border in Genoa. It was slightly less manic and she had time to exercise her poor Italian on the locals. John often interjected, to assist in any way possible to help smooth the conversations. She announced her pregnancy a few months after their return and both were overjoyed. Jessica, their first child, was born early the following spring.

Life was pretty uneventful for the next few years and things seemed to follow a predictable routine. She felt very comfortable with her lot and John was the perfect husband.

John had secured a job at a large multinational chemical company. It was a junior post, but he saw potential for future advancement. Working hard he soon caught the eye of senior management where he was encouraged to attend both internal and external courses which could only benefit both him and the company.

Five years had passed and he was on the top salary grade for his post. Life was good. A detached home and a fair-sized garden, a small family saloon stood on the drive. They had a foreign holiday every year and were even able to save a modest amount each month.

And then, ten years ago there was the accident in which four people's lives would change forever, in the blinking of an eye.

She had decided to pick John up from the railway station unannounced. They only lived a quarter of a mile away and he normally walked the short journey home. On impulse Maureen had picked up the car keys from the mantelpiece and shouted to Jessica, "Let's go and pick up Daddy!" She was elated, the test had proved positive and she was pregnant again. She was to tell John that evening.

His thirtieth birthday was only a few days away and she had planned a surprise party with a few friends invited for drinks.

She drove the short distance to the station through the light drizzle, arriving to find that the train had arrived early. That was a first! She realized John must be on his way home so she completed a U-turn in the station car park in double quick time and headed back to their house. She had only travelled a couple of hundred yards when she saw him on the other side of the road. Parking the car about twenty yards ahead she leapt out of the car and opened the passenger door allowing the excited Jessica to leave the vehicle.

She remembered feeling slightly foolish, they were only a short distance from their front door and there she was about to offer her husband a lift. She called across the road loudly to attract his attention. He looked surprised at first and then broke out into a broad grin and began to wave.

It was at that fatal moment that Jessica broke free from her mother's grasp and darted between two parked cars towards her daddy.

Doreen Carter, the local lollipop lady, was travelling in the same direction as Maureen towards the local supermarket. She was adhering to the 30 mph speed limit as she always did, she had to set an example, she had no time for the speed merchants. The very moment the diminutive Jessica appeared in view between the two parked cars, Doreen pressed the 'on' button of her car radio tucked in the centre console.

In the one second of distraction the lollipop lady's car had travelled forty-four feet and Jessica was underneath the braking car. She never regained consciousness and died the next day. The case against Doreen Carter never reached court as it was deemed unsafe. Apparently she has never driven since.

Needless to say there was no birthday party and the joyous announcement of the pregnancy was delayed until a suitable moment arrived.

The feelings of guilt were relentless and continued for months. John never forgave himself for waving and considered it was a green light for Jessica to come to him. Maureen, on the other hand, blamed herself for making the decision to pick up her husband and not letting him walk the short distance, but most of all she could not forgive herself for releasing Jessica's hand.

The birth of Amanda lifted spirits and brought back smiles of pleasure but John was never the same again. After a period of compassionate leave from his company he returned to work and totally immersed himself in his job. Within six months he was offered European Sales and a share option. His language skills had tipped the balance over the other candidates as he was expected to make monthly trips to the European capitals in which there were offices.

Maureen could have travelled to some of these exciting places with John but had elected to stay at home, never letting Amanda out of her sight, restricting her development potential, which caused her acute embarrassment as she grew older.

John's salary had quadrupled over the last few years and they had moved to a village just a couple of miles away. The house stood in its own grounds with half an acre of land and an adjoining field which they rented, enabling Amanda's pony to graze and occasionally carry her over small obstacle jumps that had been strategically placed, but were woefully small in height, to minimise the chances of an accident. The large farmhouse kitchen was graced by a mandatory Aga stove. And a cleaner was employed for cash on three mornings a week. John's large German saloon car stood gleaming on the gravel drive and a local boy was paid to wash and polish the vehicle most weekends. Maureen had elected to travel locally by taxi for most of her short journeys, having developed a deep-seated dislike for the motor car. All the food shopping was done online using the family computer and the supermarket delivery van was a regular sight coming to the house.

Things carried on much the same as the years rolled by until John started to develop headaches which grew progressively intense and more regular. Initially aspirin and then painkillers were taken with some success. He had begun to be increasingly short-fused over trivial matters and a visit to the doctor's was suggested. This was refused at first until the pain became more intense and an appointment was made. The doctor decided that the way forward was an MRI scan and then to act on the results.

What appeared to be a small tumour pressing on the brain was the culprit and the information was received with grave foreboding. This was made even worse over the next few weeks when further tests revealed that the growth was malignant and an operation was deemed impossible.

The countdown to the inevitable had begun. The mood in the house was dark and grim as the reality of the situation sank in that John was going to die, and it would be sooner rather than later.

He stopped going to work, but before doing so had a few meetings with senior management to discuss his final salary and pension rights. There were no celebrations when he left, just a shaking of the hands with eyes glued to the floor and a complete feeling of dejection, as the managing director thanked him for all his efforts and wished his family well.

Before the various painkillers and drugs took over virtually all aspects of John's life he had locked himself away in his study making numerous phone calls to various people and generally putting his financial house in order and securing their future. He had written a letter addressed to Maureen to be opened after his death explaining his funeral wishes. He was just not up to a debate.

"Well you know the rest," said Maureen wearily to her sister, but decided to continue. John had died mercifully in his sleep in the early hours of Saturday morning, the deterioration of his health had been dramatic that week so it came as no surprise. The funeral was arranged for the following Friday and his wishes adhered to. All except one, that is. It was John's fervent request that he should be buried in the same plot as Jessica with the option of his wife also being buried there, subject to her not remarrying.

This idea was soon dashed by the undertakers, as it was sensitively explained that three burials in one plot were no longer allowed under health and safety directions. Apparently digging graves to a depth of well over two metres had occasionally been the subject of accidents with the side walls collapsing while excavating. Indeed, worse had happened at funerals when lowering the coffin into the depths.

A way out was offered in that two coffins and a cremation urn for Maureen would be acceptable. Maureen decided that there was no rush to make a decision about her future interment and graciously left.

The house and grounds and all the contents would naturally become hers and this was in the hands of the family lawyers.

It was the same with all the investments and savings. Maureen revealed to Pamela that the painting in the hall of

Two Songbirds at Dawn by an up-and-coming artist should be given to her as John had noticed her coveting the canvas on her visits. Maureen candidly admitted that the painting was "not her cup of tea", and that Pamela could gladly have it when they returned to the house, stating her reluctance to the purchase in the first place and the "awful waste of money".

Maureen slipped her arm through Pamela's and asked to be walked back to Pamela's car. "Could we pop by Amanda's school on the way to the house," she said. "I know we are early but I don't like to worry her." Pamela nodded and they moved back a step.

Maureen hesitated then stopped abruptly. "The solicitor's office phoned this morning asking me to see Andrew Snell, one of the partners, around 3pm on Monday. They were a bit vague on the phone but about twelve years ago John began to put the maximum into one of those tax-free vehicles which he considered a good bet, and eventually there was quite a sum involved. Well three months ago, or thereabouts, John cashed in this part of his portfolio transferring it into his current account and then withdrawing it later as cash. He dealt with all the major financial matters as you know, as he was extremely meticulous about such things and that was one thing less for me to worry about. It seems that they can't locate the money at the moment but I am sure that it will turn up."

Pamela looked quizzically at Maureen and then asked the obvious question. "How much are they talking about,

Maureen?" "With interest about £50,000," replied Maureen blandly. "Come on, let's go."

Chapter Two

The urban fox scampered through the graveyard looking for a late afternoon snack. Its staple diet was the earthworm and he was hoping for a small feast before the ground became too hard under a winter's sky and the strong possibility of a night frost. He had mated several times with a local vixen that week as it was January, the only time of the year when she could become pregnant. If successful the cubs would be born in the spring, a time of plenty, he hoped.

It was not without some scientific reasoning that graves were so deep, it was this metre of earth that kept the foxes burrowing down into the depths and causing all sorts of misery to relatives of the deceased. It was a known fact that if any dead meat was placed in the ground to a depth of a few inches then 'Reynard's' snout would find it on his nightly scavengings.

These facts would be of little interest to Franchesca Callioni as she stood looking down at the grave of John Sledge. She carried no flowers, no cards, only a handbag and her good self. I was in my little niche only a couple of yards away and knew instantly that my services would not be needed.

Franchesca started to move to and from the grave muttering under her breath. It was not possible to interpret all these utterings so these facts are not all absolute and would therefore not hold up in a court of law. Nevertheless I have tried to paint a picture as accurate as possible under the circumstances, but must admit that when the grave was left by the participants, I have no idea whether the plan was actually played out, or not, but have had to introduce some poetic licence to events since they never returned to the grave again. Franchesca was stunning. She was tall and elegant, her auburn hair cascading over her shoulders. Her forehead, nose and cheeks were in perfect balance, leading down to a full mouth and medium chin, supported by a slender female neck without a hint of a crease. She wore a black trouser suit with matching shoes, a red silk scarf adding the final touch, held in place by a gold clasp... An Italian beauty. By her side, dressed in a black leather jacket and white polo neck, with a pair of expensive jeans to match, was the slender figure of her brother Fredo. He seemed to be the reluctant participant in the deceit that was to be played out with military-like planning by his sister.

He knew that Franchesca and John Sledge were more than just work colleagues, in fact they had become lovers about a year after his daughter's tragic death.

Her full title of Personal Assistant to the European Executive of Corporate Sales was as grand as they came. Too big for any name badge which was shortened to read PA Euro Sales Exec. Quite a title for quite a woman. She was brilliant at her job especially organizing John's working brief. She was the force behind his successful conferences, the choice of hotels, eateries and the local nightlife tailoring each client to what she believed was their tastes. A few exploratory phone calls to her opposite number in business had paid off in spades.

John had called a sales conference in Lisbon with Franchesca dealing with all the administration and book-ing the entire third floor of a splendid hotel in the capital. It went off without a hitch and she agreed to see him afterwards for a romantic evening in a riverside restaurant to celebrate. Apart from John having a severe headache which later cleared they had a wonderful time together culminating with a nightcap and sex in his hotel room.

Afterwards as they lay in bed John got up and went to the wardrobe and opened one of his suitcases, out of which he pulled a small briefcase. "To be opened on your birthday," he said, "and not a day before," returning to the wardrobe to retrieve a small envelope out of his suit jacket pocket. "The combination to the briefcase is in here, but you must promise me that you won't look until it is your birthday. I know I can trust you," he added.

"You're a tease, John Sledge," she remembered saying, kissing him softly on the cheek. The next day after dealing with some last-minute tedium they took a hire car and travelled to one of the many wine lodges, returning in time for his flight home. It was the last time that she would see him.

On his return he telephoned her continuously, but the calls became shorter and shorter, complaining constantly of this pounding in his skull which was getting worse by the day.

A fortnight before her birthday he phoned her and between stifled sobs explained about the tumour and the fact it was inoperable and that the future looked short and bleak. Through crushing pain he had told her he loved her and that this was to be his last call to her. This was not the case, as a few days later he phoned her again, and she cried, as he rambled on in an incoherent fashion, lapsing in and out of rational conversation.

The following week the managing director had phoned her and told her of John's death. He would contact her again after the funeral to discuss her future. No, she hadn't made up her mind about attending the funeral, citing her ailing father as an escape route. She did not attend the funeral, but sent a simple floral wreath with the words: John Sledge, a fine man, much missed, Franchesca.

She awoke on the morning of her birthday and immediately broke down in tears. She had been thinking of John and the lovely times they had shared and then in the next second realized he was no more. She would make a coffee and then open the briefcase. Her hands were shaking as she stumbled about looking for the envelope which held the code to the combination lock. She couldn't find it. "Damn," she thought, as she stared at the heavy black case she had placed on the table adjacent to her bed. She remembered the night of the sales conference and the small drop of red wine that spilt on her immaculate jacket. Not enough to spoil the evening, but just sufficient to jog her memory afterwards that it needed a trip to the dry cleaners. That is where she had placed the envelope.

A quick call to the shop and her worst fears were realized. Yes, they had the jacket, yes, they had found the tiny envelope inside a pocket that was cunningly stitched into the main aperture and easily overlooked. She gave the assistant an order to open the envelope and retrieve the paper inside. The chemicals used in the cleaning process had caused the ink to run. "It is all undecipherable blue squiggles," the assistant blurted. Franchesca had not scolded the girl for not searching the garment more thoroughly before processing, but thanked her, told her she would come into the shop later in the week, and put the phone down.

The phone rang almost immediately and the voice of Fredo was heard on the other end, wishing her a happy birthday in tones reminiscent of a child. For a moment she forgot her dilemma and thanked him warmly. "What are you doing this lunchtime?" she asked him. He replied that he had not made any plans at the moment. "Can you pop round about midday," she asked, "and bring a hammer, chisel and hacksaw?" she said as an afterthought.

Fredo arrived at the stroke of noon carrying the burglar kit with a stout screwdriver as a back-up. As head of the town's main art gallery, getting the time off was easy and anyway he was a little intrigued by the unknown task he was about to perform. "This is a present from John Sledge," Franchesca had told Fredo, "and I have mislaid the combination," she explained. "I would like you to break into it for me."

After spending some fifteen minutes gently prodding the case from all angles Fredo realized that a more robust attack was needed. With Franchesca's blessing he had set about the combination lock with the hammer and chisel. Within five minutes of hefty striking, the combination lock fell onto the floor, a mangled mess. Next came the retaining finger clips which were surprisingly more difficult until they gave way under the pressure of the screwdriver. They both stared at the damaged case, panting for breath, him with exertion, her with excitement. They both noticed that the lid of the case was loose and ready to be opened. "Would you like me to leave?" Fredo offered politely. "No, stay," she had retorted, "I am dying to know what is inside."

She opened the lid gently to expose a sheet of bubble wrap which was gently removed to reveal a bulging case of bank notes. They were all in small bundles, fifty of them, a thousand pounds to the bundle. "Fifty grand," blurted Fredo.

The next couple of hours were spent in discussion until Franchesca masterminded a plan. Keeping the money was out of the question. She could not keep it, she stated. "I would feel unclean, a whore, I loved him for himself not for the money, I gave myself to him gladly. The money has to go back to his family," she said firmly, ignoring Fredo's protestations.

"How the hell are you going to do that," blurted Fredo, sinking into a chair, "without his wife knowing?"

A cold chill brought her back to the graveyard staring at her brother. "Let me go through the plan one last time," she said, fixing her stare on the shaking Fredo. "We have one hour."

"It was on one of his business trips when I asked John if he would like to go to Fredo's art gallery for a private view. It was there that he had spotted a painting by an Italian who had mastered his craft under the tutelage of one of Italy's great portrait painters. The painting was on loan to the gallery and John had asked Fredo if he would act as a go-between and try to secure it for him."

After some lengthy discussions the price had been agreed at 59,000 euros or sterling equivalent. The purchase was to be a surprise and John had to raise the cash while Fredo sought, and got, an export licence.

Everything was going swimmingly until Fredo received a phone call from John. A month before he had brought the cash over on one of his business trips and left it in Fredo's safekeeping, but now the medical problems were stacking up and he was not sure if his health would improve. He had asked if the deal could be cancelled on medical grounds and the money returned.

Fredo had managed to pacify the artist and still retain the money. He had obtained John's home address from Franchesca and as he was coming to England he had decided to bring the money personally and offer his condolences.

Franchesca held out her hand to Fredo. "Perfect," she said. "Drop me off at the railway station in the hire car and then go to John's house, Maureen will be home by now. I will see you at the hotel later this evening and then we will fly back home tomorrow."

Fredo Callioni pressed the doorbell of Maureen Sledge's house and the rhythmic chimes rang out. A curtain twitched momentarily and then returned. "Who is it?" shouted Maureen nervously. "I am Fredo Callioni, brother of Franchesca Callioni, a friend of your late husband John, I have something that may be of interest to you, will you open the door?"

Submarine

Chapter One

Silent as the grave the barn owl glided through the cemetery. Its numbers have decreased over the years due to the loss of available nesting sites such as Dutch barns and hay lofts. Coupled with this, the removal of hedgerows have made homes for small rodents on which they feed more scarce.

Unlike on agricultural land, organochlorine insecticides were not in use on the several acres of the graveyard so there were rich pickings to be had for this handsome predator. It was easily identified by its large head, short, square tail and medium-long wings, beautifully coloured orange-buff above with grey vermiculation and a pure white breast.

Heading for his home in the church bell tower which was situated in the vast expanse of the graveyard, he remained unobserved by the half a dozen young men clustered around the grave of Robin Round. There was something unusual about the gathering which was not immediately discernible and then it became blatantly obvious, all the men were exactly the same height.

Luckily, the group were only a few yards from me when one of them told a man, known only as 'Smudge', that water was needed to fill up the vase that they had brought with them. The pink carnations could then be utilized once the polythene wrap was removed.

Within a minute I was amidst the group and could hear every word. Maybe the nagging mystery of why these men were not at the funeral of Robin Round, some three months before, would be resolved. I was eager with anticipation.

It soon became apparent that the leader of the group who was addressed as 'Chalkie', was acting on behalf of others who could not be there.

They had met at an agreed time at the Nelson public house which was a few hundred yards from the entrance to the graveyard and sank a couple of pints before walking to the cemetery, picking up the flowers and vase from a seller outside using the proceeds of a kitty of which Chalkie was in charge.

I listened intently as the story unfolded and all became clearer as I tried to unravel the mystery.

They were all submariners and had been on exercise and patrol in the North Atlantic and other parts for the best part of two months. It was on the way to the exercise that Robin Round had died. Due to the strict secrecy of the mission they could not return to base and the body was transferred at sea on to a frigate and a replacement crew member brought on board by helicopter.

It was a lucky break that they were not carrying nuclear missiles at the time, which under the code of operations did not allow them to surface and make radio contact, otherwise the body would have been stored in the large freezer for the duration of the trip and no replacement would have been possible.

It all started without fuss when the crew left Faslane naval base in Scotland. The submarine was manned by two crews, alternating 'off' and 'on' duty. The 'on' group on that fateful journey were Chalkie's mob and were called 'Port Watch', the other group, called 'Starboard Watch', were left on land to take leave, go on courses, tidy up the base and the like.

Port Watch were distinctly focused on their tasks as they headed out into the open sea and a rendezvous with a naval task force. The delicate job of negotiating the shallows had been accomplished and they were heading into the Atlantic Ocean to a designated point, south of the Labrador Sea off the coast of Greenland. There the war games would begin.

After a two-hour sail the captain gave the order to

"dive" and the aft hydroplanes, controlling the angle of descent, came into play, allowing the submarine to slip below the waves.

It would take the best part of two days to reach the rendezvous point and the pressure on the crew lifted slightly as they entered their secret underwater world.

A British nuclear submarine is quite a beast and is a lot bigger than most people think. A lot smaller than its American and Russian counterparts which ran to almost 300 metres in length, it is still a formidable weapon, and with enough firepower to scare most surface vessels.

Taking a trip round the boat from the sharp end back to the propellers there are the front torpedo tubes with half a dozen at the ready with a few spares standing by if needed. The forward hydroplanes are also housed there.

Immediately behind the deadly cargo and on the upper deck is one of two accommodation rooms with the dining area immediately behind them.

Underneath the front accommodation lies an area packed with machinery, with the boat's stores next door.

Amidships and beneath the giant conning tower bristling with antennae and search-and-attack periscopes sits the control room and nerve centre of the submarine. Next to this and on the same level is the nuclear power plant emitting a gentle hum which does little to portray the immense potential which lies inside this secret leviathan.

Underneath this, surprisingly, is more accommodation for the crew in which they spend many happy stand-down hours. They have all undergone intense psychological profile tests so any major squabbles are highly unlikely, which is just as well considering the long weeks of confinement in such a relatively small space.

To the rear of this and taking up the space of two levels was a large area affectionately known as Sherwood Forest. This was the home of the sixteen missiles which were kept on board and in a state of readiness.

Finally, at the blunt end of the submarine was located the rear hydroplanes which controlled the angle of dive. Last but not least was the all-important rudder which steered her.

In case of emergency, both forward and aft, escape hatches were fitted.

So this was the state of affairs as Port Watch, under Captain David Armstrong, set out for three days of exercise somewhere off Greenland, to be followed by an undisclosed patrol of over two months' duration, remaining submerged at all times.

Chalkie began to recite the events leading up to the death of Robin to the submariners huddled around his grave. They had all been there save for the captain but Chalkie felt obliged to cover the chain of events because he had a nagging feeling that something was not quite right with the explanation of Robin's death although there was nothing pointing to the contrary.

They had all gone about their duties in a professional manner, checking and rechecking equipment. Robin had a special brief to keep the machinery room shipshape at all times as this was deemed to be a place where an accident was liable to happen if equipment was not properly stowed.

It was on day two of the voyage, when the submarine was darkened to assimilate night-time, that some of the crew gathered after the evening meal for a game of cards. Time to relax for a moment while others steered the boat.

Robin left the group for a final check of the machine room while above in the control room the captain gave the order to "up periscope". All that could be seen in the panoramic sweep of the ocean was a lone fishing boat which was some two miles distant. Another sweep and the scope was retracted. All was well, the sea was theirs and it was time for a cuppa. Tomorrow the crew would be put through their paces in a series of tests to prove their readiness for the exercise which involved many ships from various allied navies.

It was about an hour later, Chalkie explained, that without warning there was a huge judder felt throughout the submarine. The whole episode lasted no longer than twenty seconds but it felt like an hour.

A series of events followed that were large in number yet simultaneous. The pitch of the engines rose and fell briefly like a giant hand had grasped the submarine and then released it. Likewise the hum of the nuclear plant rose, spiked, and fell back into the safety zone.

All crew that were seated were thrown sideways in their chairs, some holding tight, others slithering onto the floor. Those that were standing suffered a worse fate, as the boat slowed momentarily, so did they and then their inertia carried them forward crashing hard into objects but only receiving minor injuries.

The captain ordered the silencing of the collision alarm and demanded damage reports from all areas of the boat. I remembered Robin had gone to the machine room and I scrambled down there to see if he was all right, choked Chalkie.

Robin had received a massive blow to the temple from a huge vice which was bolted to the steel work bench. His mouth was gaped and his eyes were wide open, staring at the ceiling with a shocked look as if he had seen the devil. He was as dead as a dodo.

There would be no rest that night, nor the following day, as systems were checked and rechecked for operational worthiness.

Captain Armstrong studied his operational brief in fine detail and was sure, given the facts, that he could break radio silence and contact a British navy frigate explaining the situation and asking for the body of Able Seaman Round to be transferred to them and a replacement to be ferried aboard, preferably with communications experience. He stated that the sub was sound, that they would be taking part in the exercise and would continue on patrol afterwards for the duration of the mission.

Some two hours later a reply was received from the frigate. They were to rendezvous that night at a given place and time and Robin would be taken off the submarine. A replacement would be flown out from Faslane base to Greenland and then helicoptered to the given coded coordinates after the completion of the exercise.

The transfer of anything at sea was perilous, but at night that complicated things and the last thing he wanted was another accident.

Robin's body had been stowed in a body bag, but not before the captain had said a few words over the deceased in front of all hands. In the hectic few hours that followed, he had given orders to make ready for the rendezvous with the frigate, explained to the crew that he believed that the submarine had been involved in a collision with a trawl net and that the outer structure of the sub had sustained only minor damage. Injuries to the crew, except for Robin, were mostly superficial and resulted in minor cuts and bruises. Orders were given to scan for the trawler as it was not beyond the bounds of possibility that it had been pulled under by the encounter. It was discovered almost immediately chugging along with all its night lights clearly visible.

The submarine surfaced around midnight within a few hundred yards of the frigate. The body was placed gingerly into a small inflatable boat and transferred to the frigate. Robin's personal effects and private details were also despatched in a kit bag. Unknown to the crew at the time Robin would be transferred again to a support vessel after the exercise to be home in Blighty within a week. The exercise ran as smooth as silk and the submarine would be released a few hours early as all expectations of the boat and crew had been realized. This gave Captain Armstrong valuable time to pick up the new hand. 'Smudge' Roberts had been contacted at his home address and was told to report to Faslane base without fuss. He was told only that he would be away from home for about two months and that was all.

On arrival at the base he was given two one-way tickets, one was a rail pass to Glasgow and the other a flight ticket to Nuuk in Greenland where he would be met by a navy chopper pilot.

The meeting went ahead and he was soon winging his way to a point ten miles south of Cape Farewell, just off the south coast of Greenland.

The chopper pilot and winch man worked together like true professionals and Smudge soon found himself on the deck of the submarine. "The Brits certainly know how to organize things," thought Smudge. In fifteen minutes he was on board, introduced to the crew, and the boat submerged. The submarine headed north up the Denmark Strait and it was then, between the coasts of Greenland and Iceland, that the captain opened his sealed orders for their patrol over the coming weeks. The defence of the nation was their prime directive as they lurked unseen and unheard beneath the waves.

At the graveside Chalkie began to recount some anecdotes of events that had happened on land and sea with Robin Round. To raise the spirits of those assembled, he reminded them in true naval humour of the time Robin volunteered to change the oil and filter in one of the ratings' cars. He had secured the maintenance pit for half an hour and when driving onto the open pit he remembered, too late, that the car was a three-wheeler. The front end crashed down into the pit, wedging the sides with himself trapped. He received a mighty dressing-down from 'God' for that, and a hefty bill from his mate, which after a cooling-off period and several pints, was dropped. The dark humour continued when he reminded all present that on that fateful night, as Robin went to the machine room, he had been dealt a full house at poker which spilled on to the floor on impact with the trawl net. Bloody rotten luck, Chalkie said, with just the hint of a grin.

Finally, said Chalkie, the captain sends his apologies, top brass called him down to London – some sort of inquiry, he said.

"Oh I forgot! When we go back to Faslane all of you will do the rounds, no pun intended, for Robin's wife, and no coins accepted!"

Chapter Two

The long-tailed tit had picked a fork high up in a tree adjacent to the grave of Robin Round in which to build a nest. Of the group of tits belonging to the Parus family – the great, blue, coal and marsh tits, only the long-tailed tits have both male and female to build their nest. For the rest of the group only the skill of the female is used. It was just as well that they worked together as the whole structure took some three weeks to build, and used over two thousand feathers in the lining alone.

The cock and the hen glared down silently at the two men by the graveside who were unaware that they were being observed from the four-inch-high dome of the nest, brilliantly hidden above them.

"We both forgot to bring flowers," said Captain David Armstrong to the other man. "Would you mind filling the jug over there?" he said, pointing to me first and then the tap. "At least we can top up the vase, it's almost dry and the existing flowers are beginning to wilt." The task completed, I was placed gently by the graveside.

"I was ordered to HQ in London to what I thought was an inquiry into the incident that occurred just before the exercise and was greeted by a naval attaché who told me not to worry, that there had been a meeting of minds and that it was all sorted. I told him that I had arranged to come to Round's grave that day with the men to pay my respects, but he intervened and said he was sorry but coming to HQ was more important," explained Captain Armstrong.

"He gave me an envelope and told me to go back home and then go to the Royal Oak pub in Eldridge the following day where I should introduce myself to a Lance Brightman whose picture would be in the envelope. I was to be dressed casually and be there at 1300 hours sharp. Bloody cloak and dagger stuff!"

Lance took over. "Well that was a couple of hours ago, and now we are here. I think I've got a bit of explaining to do and didn't want to say much in the car as I'd explain all in due course.

"First of all let me tell you that I have been down at

your HQ with others for the past two days and been subject to quite a grilling.

"Yes, I am Lance Brightman, but when I am earning my keep for the good old US of A, I am Commander Brightman of the US nuclear sub *Altona*, and I am also responsible for the death of that poor seaman buried down there," he said, pointing to the grave of Robin Round.

"Responsible," said Armstrong, "responsible," he said again, louder. "How?"

Commander Brightman continued. "We were on the joint ops but had arrived a couple of days early and took shelter in one of those deep underwater canyons. Our mission was to come out undetected when the exercise was in full flow and throw a spanner in the works, so to speak.

"Well, it all got a bit tight down there, so I gave the order to come out of our hidey-hole and rig for silent running. It was a few moments after this that you were passing by on your way to the exercise, and we had left the canyon when the unthinkable happened.

"Initially I thought we had scraped along one of those rocky canyons, losing a detection antenna for our trouble, but suffered no structural damage or casualties. It was later when we intercepted your communication to the frigate that your submarine had apparently come into contact with a trawler net and that a seaman was fatally injured that I knew we had been involved in a 'coming together' of the two subs.

"I must be honest with you, David," continued Lance, "that my first reaction was to keep the episode 'hush-hush', have the antenna replaced and the superficial damage to the hull repaired. Obviously the top brass back in the States would know, and that would be it. My idea was backed by my superior officers, realizing that a statement releasing the true facts would be too embarrassing to admit. You know how it would look – banner headline – 'American and British submarines collide in Atlantic exercise'. Well that would have been the end of the sorry tale until it came out in a Pentagon brief and the Secretary of State got wind of it.

"It was decided that the subtle art of deception could not be played out on a staunch ally, and a plot was hatched on a need-to-know basis.

"The need-to-know was my Secretary of State, your Defence Secretary, and me and you. No crew members would know the true facts and the brush with a trawler net would stand."

"What about Able Seaman Round's wife?" blurted Dave Armstrong, his face portraying his shock at learning the truth.

"Well, that's been sorted out as well," replied Lance. "I have been briefed fully and I am acting with the joint agreement of both governments. They considered it would be better that it came from me, but if you wish to clarify any points, I have the direct number of Rupert Johnson at your Ministry of Defence. I'm sure you have heard of him.

"If you let me finish, Dave, all will be revealed and we might get a chance to try a pint of your good old fashioned British beer before I return stateside.

"They thought long and hard about compensating Robin Round's wife, but decided that there was nothing that could be done without raising suspicion. Anyway, she would receive a generous lump sum and lifetime pension from your naval department. However, to compensate for our guilt, further research was undertaken and it was discovered fortuitously that the Rounds have a son, Mark, who is considered quite a talent, especially in the field of computer sciences. He is to be offered a two-year open scholarship at Massachusetts Institute of Technology which they are sure he will accept. He will be made for life, David. That's one good thing that has come out of this, don't you agree?"

David acknowledged Lance with a grunt and Lance continued.

"As for me, that's a different matter. Although they agreed that leaving the canyon was a decision that was made on safety grounds, and mine to make alone, it was deemed that if I had stopped within the canyon walls for the predetermined length of time, then the accident would not have happened. I am being transferred to the submarine warfare and training school in Boston, Mass., without loss of rank and my record unblemished. As a rider to this and a valid point, they pointed out that my crew would not be in a position to ask any questions which might put me in a difficult spot. A transfer would put paid to that and it would soon become a distant memory to them."

David Armstrong absent-mindedly picked me up and while returning me to my normal position his mobile phone rang.

"Armstrong," the voice said with an authoritative air, "Rupert Johnson, Ministry of Defence, are you still with Brightman?" Without waiting for a reply he continued, "Just been reading the Greenland exercise reports. Excellent performance, David! They need someone like you down at the Admiralty. An ideas man. It's a promotion of course, you start Monday next. Some of your chaps have been putting two and two together and coming out with five. Best you have a desk job for a while. I know you'll understand. Rear Admiral Chivers is your contact." The phone went dead. David Armstrong turned to face Lance Brightman. "Are you ready for that pint, Lance? I think I am!"

VOLUME II

A Message from the Secret Jug

I have been poorly, very poorly, with injuries hard for humans to understand. I can only liken it to you having broken your leg or any limb. Pain, and shock, in large measures.

I offer no apology, my friends, for not recounting more tales for your enjoyment, but I have been unable to do so. Let me explain.

Sometime a few weeks ago, or was it months, I really don't know, it was then it happened. It was not an accident or a mindless act of vandalism that caused my pain, but the weather. A period of unrelenting rain allowed water to drip into me, even though I am in a place of comparative shelter.

The water rose to a fairly high level. Normally this is no problem as I am a conveyance of the life-giving fluid, but a sharp frost followed, allowing the temperature to drop well below freezing. When the thaw came, there was a sudden crack and I felt ill. I was holed below the water line.

Not only was I injured, but also my usefulness as a water carrier was gone. No longer did people pick me up and take me to the water tap and then to their graves to top up or replenish their flower vases. I had become useless.

Time passed, endless and foggy tracks of time, and then I was jolted from my cataleptic state. I was lifted, and taken complete with my broken parts and taken to the home of my benefactor. Over the days I was painstakingly repaired and my damaged parts superglued back together. When the final piece was set and secured I undertook an amazing transformation.

I became fully conscious, aware that all the pain had gone and was now back to my old self, save for a few visible repair lines. It was hard to stop quivering with delight. I was *alive*.

A few days later I was taken back to the cemetery and placed in the nook adjacent to the grave of John Chmara. I noticed a few changes, there were new graves, fresh flowers and the odd plastic milk bottle dotted about, used presumably in my absence. I was now back in business, awaiting customers with tales to tell.

Stand by for three new yarns from the pen of the Secret Jug.

Bad Boy

Chapter One

The two young men walking up the path towards me were new to yours truly, as they strolled towards a newish grave of Roger Ledger.

By the loud language it soon became apparent that the alpha male was Jason Ledger and the quiet one Simon Ledger. The grave was some twenty yards distant, but even so I felt a feeling of unease and trepidation, which I can report was not without justification.

I noticed that the pair were empty-handed as they approached, so I was surprised when Jason, the older of the two, ordered his brother to "get that jug from that grave over there, and go fill it with water from that tap near the path."

Simon turned to question this command because they had not brought any flowers, but his brother had gone, and was heading for another part of the cemetery, which was situated on the other side of the path. Nevertheless, Simon carried out the order and came towards me lifting me with gentle hands, filling me with water from the tap, and then returned to the grave. A couple of minutes later Jason returned clutching a bunch of chrysanthemums that had seen better days and an old plastic vase, the type with a tapered base.

Simon was flabbergasted but still asked the lame question as to where he had got the two items. It was obvious that they had been taken from another grave some distance away.

"They won't know where their stuff has gone," said Jason, thrusting the vase into the soft earth at the side of the grave and then popping in the flowers, one at a time into the vase. Finally water was filled up to the brim. "Job done," said Jason, discarding me with a flick of his hand into the grass nearby. Fortunately, I remained intact but severely shaken. What a lout this man is, I thought, wondering how this nightmare would end.

It was then for the first time that I noticed that the headstone was etched like no other I had seen. It was simply inscribed:

ROGER LEDGER 2018

I subsequently discovered that this was Jason's idea. Lettering on the stone was charged by the number of letters used, the more you asked for the more expensive it became, and this was the bare minimum. I heard Simon remark that he was surprised that Jason had the year placed on the stone. All that was said with sneering sarcasm.

While they talked I was able to observe the two men standing uncomfortably together. Simon was just short of six feet in height, with short, cropped hair and sideburns at military level. I can only describe his face as handsome, with a generous mouth and angular chin. He wore an old brown jacket with damage to the elbows covering a rolled-neck white sweater. His trousers were brown with fade marks near the knee. The shoes were the same colour as the jacket, lace-up style, scuffed but immaculate.

Jason, on the other hand, was slightly smaller than his brother and distinctly unattractive. His long hair was straight at the back with evidence of over-gelling at the front. The face was hollow at the cheeks and the mouth thin and tight. All this with a wispy goatee beard and dark glasses, which I never saw him remove, gave the overall impression of a man on the dark side of life. It was the clothes he wore that commanded attention. He was dressed in a black leather jacket, which was made of the softest of hides, with a motif of a high-end sports car embossed on the left breast. A matching pair of small gold cuff links with a similar design was attached to the end of the sleeves. His trousers were of the same soft leather, tight-fitting round the ankle. The shoes were easy-fit, black and uncared-for.

Chapter Two

I learned that Roger Ledger worked for a public utility company. Had married his teenage sweetheart and had three children, all boys within the space of five years. Elsie was a dutiful wife who never went to work, but was happy to tend the small family home and bring up the boys in the best way she could. This was all with the blessing of her husband.

Roger's early promotion to district supervisor was not the reason for his apparent wealth. Early in his marriage he had made a decision to invest in the stock market rather than the more traditional methods of saving that suited the general populace. Bank and building society savings were too mundane for him, there was a hint of a gambler lurking beneath this ordinary fellow.

He joined a syndicate of six like-minded chaps, who met once a week in the back room of a local tavern where they spent a couple of hours poring over the week's financial news and hot tips. After all six agreeing to the purchases of the week they invested their equal amounts and the shares were duly purchased.

Their enterprise continued for the best part of ten years until a meeting was held to mutually dissolve the partnership. The accumulated wealth was now quite considerable and this led Roger to take the gamble of his life. He successfully borrowed the money required to buy out the share options of the syndicate, placing himself heavily in debt, but he owned all the shares. This situation continued for a further year until the burden of the loan, and possibility of a stock market crash, led him to sell all the shares, pay off the loan, settle the tax liabilities and bank the profits. He had made a small fortune which was to be enhanced still further when he met an old friend, who told him that his son worked in the oil fields of one of the old Russian satellite states and this embryonic company was on the verge of a major oil find. The share price was small, only a few pence, but the risk was worth it he was told. Roger was no fool and realized taking a punt from a man in a pub was fraught with danger, but he felt good about the opportunity and bought a few thousand oil shares. These he kept for two years and then sold them for a substantial profit. This left him devoid of any shares, but financially secure.

Roger and Elsie lived very well, they had a few splendid holidays, but never moved from the family home. This idyllic lifestyle continued for a few more years, until Elsie died, after a complication set in following a minor heart operation. Roger soldiered on for a few more years remaining a widower. The boys had all left home, so he planned early retirement with the prospect of wintering in the sunshine until the early signs of dementia showed its evil beginnings. It was at this time that he started to get more and more visits from his son Jason.

Suddenly I felt I was being lifted into the air. I was not worried or stressed, as it was the strong comforting hands of Simon that were taking me back to my place of rest and shelter. At the time I thought I would never see them again in this place. But I was wrong, so very wrong. They then left together.

Chapter Three

A month had passed without anything in particular occurring when Simon appeared, flowers in hand. He pulled the vase and contents from the ground walked over to the bin and emptied the old flowers into it. He then returned with the vase and carefully placed the new flowers inside it.

A thin kitchen sponge was then produced from his coat pocket, which he used to wipe down the headstone, using the remaining water to pour over the plinth. He then leant over touching the top of the headstone with his fingers and said, "Hello bro".

To say I was in a state of shock would be a complete understatement. The conversation that they held a month earlier referred to Roger, his wife Elsie, their children and a precise life story. If this person in the grave was not their father then it must be a person with the same forename. This Roger in the grave must be his brother. Simon began to speak and the mystery started to unfold, slowly at first and then a torrent of information followed.

He began by saying how much he had missed his younger brother, how he was the apple of his father's eye, who had given him his name. That he had been on an urgent training mission in the Middle East for the British Army and only had a few days' compassionate leave granted for the death of Roger Ledger senior. A tear appeared as he stated that his brother would not be lying beneath him in his coffin if he had been at home, and that the both of them being cut out of their father's will was beyond his understanding. However, he was determined to seek some answers from Jason.

Speaking of Jason he was appalled at how he had changed, stating that some of his new friends were more gangland than was good for him. "I think he has lost his moral compass," he went on to say, "he has become loud and aggressive, and how the hell did he finance that car?"

Simon's temper cooled a little as he addressed his brother in a quiet personal style. "I was sure as I can be in my own mind, that you were relying on a big slice of Dad's fortune to assist you with your business worries, to the point that it wouldn't be just a help but a necessity to be left the money. I believe your whole future depended on it. When you found out that Dad's will did not include you, it became obvious that the business would fail. The refusal of the bank to help you was the last straw, or let's say, the penultimate straw that broke the camel's back. Along with Alice leaving you it was enough to push you over the edge. That's why you did it, damn you, you poor little fool," he cried. A few minutes passed in complete silence before Simon continued to speak. "In two weeks' time it would have been your birthday, I shall meet here again with Jason to pay our respects." Simon then picked me up and returned me to my place of shelter and he was gone.

Chapter Four

A fortnight had passed and true to his word Simon arrived with fresh flowers and in need of my services. He was tidying the surrounds to the grave when Jason arrived, cruising up the avenue in his gleaming sports car and parked up. Staggering a little he made his way to the grave, Oh dear, I thought, he looks drunk.

"Well, I'm here," said Jason slurring a little. "What's the score then?" he blurted. Simon explained, "The score is that it was Roger's birthday in case you have forgotten and I need to discuss a few things with you." A conversation then took place with Simon leading the way.

He wanted to know more about the latter days of their father's illness and some kind of explanation as to why both Roger and Simon had been left out of the will. Not stopping for breath, he demanded to know how Jason had managed to achieve power of attorney over his late father's affairs, and where the bulk of the estate had disappeared.

Jason was keen to tell Simon that he had taken care of their dad but remained vague about the other questions. He said the onus of responsibility had fallen on him to care for Roger senior as Simon was away with his "darling army" and Junior was tied 24/7 with that "bloody business", and that he had no idea the workload he had taken on.

Jason continued to say, he occasionally popped into see Dad, and noticed that over time he had changed from the well-mannered, balanced individual they all knew, to a more surly, sometimes forgetful, aggressive man that Simon would not have recognized. According to Jason, he only shaved when instructed and was eating irregularly. The deterioration continued, he said, so he applied for and got, power of attorney over all his financial affairs. "Dad insisted that I was the only one who cared about him and that he was hell-bent on making a new will with me as the sole beneficiary. I protested most vigorously but he said it was his final decision on the matter and instructed me to get on with the legal side of things, which I did.

"A month or so later when I was about to seek the aid of a carer to help out, Dad left the house in a confused state and walked in front of a bus. I had him cremated and the ashes placed alongside Elsie. To be honest, his death was the best thing that could have happened and I was glad to see the back of the old bugger."

With this Simon snapped and hit his older brother once in the mouth, dislodging a tooth. Grasping Jason's lapel in a vice-like grip he drew his face close to his own.

"Listen," he snarled, "for the last two weeks I have been talking to the family solicitors and they have advised me that my suspicions were sufficient for them to delve into Dad's affairs. They informed me that the maximum amount was drawn on his current account on two occasions a week for months, and that his building society account had been closed. All monies, totalling many thousands had been transferred to guess who? The family home was up for sale for a tidy sum, and that they were awaiting further instructions. Anything to say, Jason?" he barked, releasing his handhold.

The blow must have triggered something in Jason's brain, maybe he felt guilty, we shall never know because it was short-lived, but lasted long enough for some semblance of truth to spurt out of the damaged mouth.

"OK! OK!" he said. "When I got the power of attorney and realized just how much money was involved, I got a bit greedy. I wheedled my way into Dad's mind and managed to get his PIN to withdraw the dough. Easy-peasy so far. The building society, again no problem, hence the motor," he said pointing to the avenue with a trembling hand.

"The will took a bit more thought, though. Dad could not understand why you and Junior weren't visiting him, especially 'the Chosen One'," he said, glaring at the grave. "It only took a few days when he was in one of his aggressive moods that I had the idea, or the seed of an idea planted in his mind, which was then adopted by him. He believed it was his own idea to change the will and leave me the lot, *brilliant!*

"I got Hornsby, the dodgy solicitor, to write it up for a couple of hundred quid and then a couple of mates from the club to witness it all. Another hundred to agree Dad was in sound mind at the time, which was small beer compared with the result.

"Look, it wasn't my fault that Junior took his life after learning that nothing was coming his way when Dad died. It was Alice leaving him that screwed him up, not me."

Simon drew himself up to his full height and glared down at Jason who by now had transformed back to his old cocksure self. He reached into the pocket of his old brown jacket and produced a mobile phone. He went to the contacts section, scrolled down to a name and punched it in. A voice answered. "Have you heard enough?" asked Simon.

Chapter Five

Johnny Roberts nibbled at the blunt end of a pencil as he sat in the unmarked surveillance vehicle situated in the car park next to the cemetery. He was an old hand at this game and knew how things could go wrong. It was only a year since that feedback noise from a transmitter on a wired informant had blown an operation. It wasn't that he didn't believe in technology, it was that he didn't trust it.

Turning off the recording equipment he spoke to the decision maker sitting next to him. It was he who had spoken to Simon ten days previously, who sought and got permission to use covert means to try and get Jason to spill the beans. It was also he that had spent a full day on the necessary method of approach to be adopted, and the fitting of the transmitting equipment, in such a way that Jason would not have had any inkling of the trap set for him.

Roberts wanted to know if there was sufficient evidence to incriminate Jason and have him in for questioning.

The decision maker affectionately known as 'Two Brains' had been scribbling furiously when the recording equipment was active, and had written down a number of bullet points he thought pertinent.

"His defence will use the assault as a means to drop the recording as evidence," he said. "They will say it was extracted under duress and provocation and therefore inadmissible. On the plus side, further investigations into Hornsby and the two accomplices might be useful.

"There is strong evidence here for fraud, embezzlement and coercion of a person mentally unfit. Nick the bastard!"

Roberts was a step in front of 'Two Brains' and had started the vehicle and was now moving out of the car park. Picking up a two-way radio, he ordered police constables Suggs and Bentworth, who were holed up in a van in a nearby cul-de-sac to stand by.

Chapter Six

Roberts brought the vehicle to a halt on the avenue at a spot near the grave and eyed up a bemused Jason. He introduced himself with the customary salutation and explained the reason for his arrival. Roberts continued the brief. "We have reason to believe that you, Jason Ledger, were involved with the unlawful…" He got no further when the accused made a bolt for his car. Fumbling with the ignition keys he bought the beast to life. Wheels spinning, he began to traverse the avenue. "See you in hell, Simon," was the farewell gift as he drove away. "See you in hell, Jason," was the soft reply.

Turning to Roberts, the decision maker made a contribution. "Might need to freeze a bank account or two," he said, thinking out loud. "Oodles of cash involved, which might mean confiscation of his passport. It looks like we could have a runner here." Roberts gave his colleague a half-look and smiled. He appreciated the words of advice but he hadn't got his prey in the interview room just yet, never mind the dock. He picked up the two-way radio, gazing at the dust trail that Jason was leaving in his wake.

Roberts barked out an order. "Suggs, Bentworth, block the exit to the cemetery. Red sports job. Arrest the driver for dangerous driving in a graveyard, his name is Jason Ledger."

Roberts turned to the decision maker and casually remarked, "I hope he stops, you know what Suggs is like with a bad boy."

Golf Ball

Chapter One

The bulldozer had been and gone, only a few items of small plant were left dotted about waiting for collection. The cemetery was in need of expansion so a small area one acre in size was purchased just north of my position. The existing wrought-iron railings, which marked the old boundary, were removed and replaced in their new setting and finally given a lick of paint. The new plot was already grassed over so only cutting was required. A few trees and bushes had to be removed from the site while others were allowed to remain for aesthetic reasons. The old avenue roadway had been extended from just up from the water tap to the end of the new acquisition, and a small vehicular turning circle added.

The old symmetry of the cemetery was lost when the railings were repositioned, leading to local opposition to the plans. The council's argument that the old graveyard was nearly full and that extending the grounds were the only viable option won the day.

A parcel of land measuring some 70 x 70 yards does not seem much in the great scheme of cemetery acquisition, but with careful planning over 600 new graves could be eventually sited there. One added bonus was that the piping to the water tap was not extended into the new plot, so that the only means of conveying water was from the existing tap, where I lay.

The dice were then rolled again in my favour when at the south end of the new development and within earshot a brand new grave was being excavated. A few days later the funeral took place with over a hundred mourners. Fine clothes mean little at such a time but the expensive apparel of all in attendance struck me. By the subdued tones of the gathering and some snippets of conversation, I knew that another complex tale was about to unfold. When the service had ended and all the people had filtered away, only two people were left grieving at the graveside. They were the children of Archibald Fairfax, Polly and Angus. "Dad wouldn't be lying here if it had not been for that bloody game of golf a year since," Polly said tearfully. "It was the catalyst to a whole chain of events that eventually killed him," she continued. "You know I'm right. The whole thing got blown up out of all proportion. Two grown men refusing to back down over a ruddy golf ball, it's beyond belief."

Chapter Two

Paxton Grange was one of the finest golf courses in the British Isles and boasted a magnificent Georgian clubhouse with joining fees and annual subscriptions in line with its prominence. Only those wealthy enough to pay the fees were members, save for the odd golfer with exceptional talent who was allowed on the course free gratis.

Of all the trophies fought over every year there was one that every member wanted his name etched on, and that was 'the Bonechester Plate', donated by Harry Bonechester some fifty years previously. Harry was a renowned philanthropist with a number of his millions set in trust for the less fortunate. A keen golfer himself, it was he that put forward this solid silver trophy for the best match play golfer of the year. It was the most prestigious event in the club's diary, and even the run-up to the final drew small crowds.

The protagonists that year were Archibald Fairfax and Christian Lampee, both playing off a handicap of seven. Archie and Chris, as they were known, were two likeable fellows who were very successful in business, and were firm friends, who often exchanged banter, which was always good-humoured. They also held exalted positions on the club committee and frequently had to make tough choices on course improvements and the purchase of machinery.

Both men had won their knockout rounds against worthy opponents and were now in the final with only room for one name on the Bonechester Plate. Angus Fairfax thought that his Dad, Archie, might just have the edge over Chris in the final, because he believed that 'big-day nerves' would unsettle Chris towards the end of the round if indeed it went that far. He sought to lay a big wager on his father, but was not sure how to do it and who would accept it. There was only one man in the club who had the reputation for such antics. Most members frowned upon gambling, as the belief was that hefty bets invariably led to strained friendships. No matter, Angus sought out Cornelius Coolman, likeable rogue and part-time bookmaker. He was also reputed to be a serious ladies' man, living alone in a country mansion only a few miles from the Grange. The source of his apparent wealth was unknown. Over a drink in the clubhouse Coolman said he would accept the bet but there would be certain provisos.

The first condition was, he sought out Christian Lampee's son David, and secured an equal wager from him. The second demand was, Cornelius would hold the bet until the outcome was known, and finally he would give them both even money odds on the result, and that they both sign presented duplicate papers to this effect.

"Angus Fairfax and David Lampee both wager £5,000 at even money on their respective fathers to win the Bonechester Plate. The wager shall be over 18 holes of golf and the money paid to the son of the outright winner at the conclusion of 18 holes."

The £5,000 bet was Angus's idea and he had no idea if David Lampee would buy into it. He need not have worried, David jumped at the chance, family honour was at stake, so he promised to bring the cash on the following Thursday with a mention that no word of this enterprise would filter back to their fathers. A final meeting was arranged with Cornelius, where two brown envelopes bulging with cash were handed over, and the duplicate papers duly signed.

Polly suggested a walk around the cemetery perimeter to get some air and warm up a little, and then to return to listen to her brother's accounts of events on the match day. As they approached, she stated that the water tap was in a convenient position to use, and at the same time she spotted *the Secret Jug* which again led to more positive comments.

"Oh, by the way," she said, "how did Corney make any money from taking such a bet?" Angus was heard to say, "Normally there would be no gain. Either he or David would pocket an extra £5,000 if their respective fathers won. But in the event of a draw at the end of the 18 holes the combatants would continue from the first tee until a hole was won. Sudden death. it's called. But our bet was over 18 holes, so if there were a drawn match at that point Cornelius would pocket the lot. Clever, hey? A draw after 18 holes happens more times than you would think." Angus added wearily, "Hindsight is an exact science, I'm told."

Chapter Three

On their return Polly seemed more relaxed and asked Angus to relive the doomed game once again. It was with a certain hesitancy that Angus spoke.

He recounted that on that fateful Saturday he was carrying his father's clubs as was David caddying for Christian. A toss of a coin allowed Archibald the honour and after a shake of hands and golf ball identification they both teed off. Both players bogeyed the first hole, which was a mixture of nerves and misreading the green. The game settled down to be a Paxton classic with birdies and bogies littering the first nine holes. A crowed of some fifty-strong had gathered to watch this golfing spectacle, enhancing the excitement of the game. They turned into the wind to face the tenth hole all square, both players exchanging pleasantries in the warm sunshine. After more fine shots and a few near misses the seventeenth tee was reached with Archie trailing by one hole. This short hole lacked distance but made up for this inadequacy by being fiendishly difficult. The hole was surrounded with bunkers and was guarded by a small pond. Christian, in a rare lack of concentration, missed the green and found a green side bunker. Archie's reply was a towering eight iron to the pin coming to rest some ten feet away. Chris played a magnificent bunker shot, which hit the flag stick but cannoned off to eight feet from the hole. It was Archie to putt first as he was the further away. His ball just lipped out of the hole followed by gasps from the crowd. The putt was conceded which I thought was fairly generous but received generous applause.

Chris needed this eight footer to halve the hole. Lining up the putt with the use of the putter shaft he addressed the ball, his face creased with deep concentration. Once the ball leaves the putter head there is nothing that can be done but to helplessly watch the path of the ball. The line was perfect but the weight of the putt was light leaving the ball one half an inch from the hole. The match was all square with only the par five eighteenth awaiting the pair. Archie had won the honour, and knew that the tables had turned in his favour, knowing that only he could reach this par five with two mighty blows whereas Chris would need three shots being the shorter hitter. The hole doglegged slightly left at the 250 yards mark and was guarded by trees all the way down the left side. Hitting the right side of the fairway and being able to view the green was a must for Archie.

Taking a deep breath he addressed the ball as a striker views a penalty kick in football. Controlled aggression was the essential ingredient required at that moment in time and Archie had it in spades.

The hushed crowd surrounded the tee box brought a touch of claustrophobia into the mix. "It was a wonderful moment," said Angus to a captivated Polly, he was so proud of his dad. As the ball flew off the mighty driver head, the future of Paxton Grange, the two players and their sons was to change forever. The golf ball travelled 250 yards through the air, on a trajectory that was 20 degrees offline, landing in a large area of rough close to the right-hand edge of the fairway. Christian walked onto the teeing area with David who handed his father a driver. Chris stated from that area of rough Archie had found, he could only hack out the ball a 100 yards at the most, so taking a three wood for safety was the wisest choice. David agreed and handed Chris the club requested. He then smoked his ball straight down the middle of the fairway.

Some of the crowd, eager to please, walked at a brisk pace towards the spot where it was thought the ball lay. Archie slow-timed his approach to the landing area hoping that the ball would be found before he arrived. He was also acutely aware that under the rules of golf, he was allowed only five minutes to find his ball from the time he arrived at the place where he thought his ball was.

On reflection he wondered if taking a provisional ball off the tee would have been a better option, but this would be classed as his third shot under the rules, and anyway, finding his golf ball should be relatively easy, so he dismissed the idea. After four minutes of searching with the help of both Chris and David, six golf balls were found but none of them carried the Titleist brand name that Archibald favoured. A wag in the crowd, probably a Lampee supporter muttered, "time, gentlemen, please" to those in earshot. Worse still, a Paxton committee member whispered to Archie that he only had thirty seconds left to find the ball. Archie was frantically thrashing about in the rough searching when, with only seconds to spare, Billy Smith, a club junior member gleefully shouted that he had found the ball. Archie raced over to the spot, his heart pounding, and identified the ball as his.

Christian and David came over to join Archie and me at the point of discovery. A conversation, began between the two players and within earshot of a few spectators. What began in a civilized fashion erupted within a few minutes to outright hostility. Chris firmly stated that Archie must be mistaken as this golf ball was ten yards or more from the projected flight path off the tee and could not be his ball. Archie retorted that the ball was indeed found in an unlikely spot, but it must have hit an old tree stump or stone deflecting it to that very spot. "Impossible," said Chris, his face beginning to flush. "The ball was at the end of its flight and couldn't cannon this far," he continued. Archie refused to budge on the matter and rotated the nestling ball in his fingers. "Look at the number," he shouted. "It's a Titleist number one, the same golf ball as I use and I am saying categorically, this is my ball."

The impasse showed no sign of resolution until Archie challenged Chris with the heart-stopping phrase, "Are you accusing me of cheating?" A full ten seconds passed until Chris replied. "If you don't concede, then yes," he said, stern-faced. "F… you, Chris Lampee," Archie replied tensely. With that they both marched up the fairway towards the clubhouse, fingers jabbing at each other, with a few spectators in hot pursuit. The only thing that David and I knew for sure on that terrible, fateful day was that Cornelius Coolman was ten thousand pounds richer.

Chapter Four

The disciplinary hearing held at the club found both players guilty of bringing the game of golf and the reputation of the club into disrepute, and they were fined £100 each. The charge of committing an unlawful act with wilful intent contravening the Rules of Golf (cheating) against Archibald Fairfax was deemed unproven. Both players were banned from the clubhouse and surrounding property owned by the club for a period of two months. The same penalty was also applied to all golf competitions for the same length of time. Both appeals made to the club were swiftly rejected. The vitriolic display witnessed and heard by members was recorded by committee members and relayed to both players at the appeals hearing, and they were also reminded that only their past exemplary conduct had prevented total exclusion from the club.

Angus pulled a handkerchief from his jacket pocket, blew hard, and turned to his sister. "Do you want me to carry on?" he asked gloomily. Polly who had been away for most of the time at university during the crisis was eager to hear more. "Tell all," was her reply. Apparently, the sports editor of the local paper, looking for a story, had approached the golf club. Only the most vague statement was released stating that on the eighteenth hole a disagreement between two players had taken place and the only course of action was to abandon the match. It was hoped that a re-match would take place in the near future.

A report on social media which was obviously 'fake news' but remained unchallenged, asserted that a player helping to search for his opponent's golf ball during the match play final on the eighteenth hole, at Paxton Grange had his putter stolen by an opportunist thief and could no longer continue. The game was abandoned. The members divided their loyalists into three camps. The Chris and Archie factions, and the impartials. All the gossip related to the match play finals, which prompted some lively debates.

On returning to the club after the expiry of the ban Archie first sighted the trophy cabinet with the Bonechester Plate taking pride of place. A quick scan down the roll of honour through the years stopped at the current year with the word 'void' inscribed.

Apparently the two members beaten in the semi-final were asked if they would play against each other for the coveted plate. After a lengthy discussion they decided it would be a pyrrhic victory to win so they both declined.

Archiebald's arrival in the club lounge was decidedly uncomfortable with half-stares and mumblings being the order of the day. The odd member went out of their way to give Archie a hearty handshake and a welcome back salutation. Strangely, the return of Christopher Lampee was received in much the same way. The worse part in all this for both players was the suspicious removal of a name from the medal starting sheets claiming injury. The most likely reason was that participating in a club competition with either of the pair might be construed as taking sides.

Chapter Five

Angus, having got his sister's full attention, decided to carry on with the grim story reverting to life at home after the golf match. Apparently not a day passed without reference to the game. Archie's wife, Denise had been supportive at first, listening attentively to her husband's tale of woe, but as the weeks turned to months the strain had become unbearable. She had booked a month's cruise in the Caribbean with her sister for a much-needed holiday. Archie felt that this was an act of desertion and became more and more withdrawn, spending large amounts of time just staring at the picture of Paxton Grange hanging above the fireplace.

Fairfax Industries, the family firm, with fifty years of experience, began to notice changes in the order books. They were tiny at first and hardly noticeable but after a few months a twenty per cent loss of orders was apparent. This was serious stuff. Archie confided that some of these customers he had known for years and were friends of the family. They had closed their accounts, without explanation and gone elsewhere. They don't want to deal with a man branded as a 'cheat', he blurted. The final ignominy and the catalyst for extreme action was the letter from the Chair of Paxton Grange suspending him from future committee meetings until further notice. No reason was given but it was obvious the golf club was still smarting from the effects of the fateful day.

Something positive needed to be done and done quickly to arrest this downward spiral of events. He retired to his den to make a lengthy phone call. On his return he exclaimed that there was no turning back now, he had instructed Barney Simpson QC to charge Christian Lampee with defamation of character, effectively a libel suit against Mr Lampee had begun.

Chapter Six

When news of this reached Paxton Grange the whole club was aghast with excitement. "More bloody press!" screamed the captain. "When will it ever stop?" He sought Christian Lampee and came straight to the point. "None of my business, Chris," he said, "but it would help the club if we knew if you were fighting this action." "You bet I am," was the reply.

After some preliminary hearings the case was heard in the high court. Both Chris and Archie refused to budge from their original positions. Over the next two days witnesses were called from both camps, and statements were read and cross-examinations made. At this point the judge stopped the trial and ordered all concerned to be back in Court for 10 o'clock the next day. The summing up was swift and decisive. He ruled in lay terms, that if they had sat till Domesday the case bought by the plaintiff could never be proved one way or the other, and the accuser's defence, was equally unsound in that both parties, knowing the evidence should have been aware of these facts. He rebuffed Archie's counsel for not being more robust with the probable outcome of the case. He found the case brought against Lampee that he defamed Archie's character unproven, and that costs, now totalling more than £100,000, be found by the plaintiff.

Paxton Grange Golf Club did not escape unscathed. He made two points directed at the club. Firstly, a rematch, when tempers had cooled, should be ordered and any participant rejecting the instructions should lose the right to claim the trophy. Secondly, a golf match of such importance should have a referee fully conversant with the rules of golf to oversee the game. Finally, his stare averting toward Archie, he stated a timeless truth, when you are unsure as to the precise position of your golf ball when playing in any club competition, play a provisional golf ball.

Chapter Seven

Angus looked at Polly, his mouth dry, and went over to the water tap to quench his thirst. On returning he addressed his sister in a solemn fashion and recounted the facts. It was his view that the accumulative effects of all that had passed from the day of the match, till the court case, and all that had happened in between led to them being there today. The illness, quickly followed by heart failure, was in a small way a blessing for Archie. "Believe me," Angus continued, "he had lost the will to carry on. He told me that the whole business had stripped him of his honour and his dignity and that he was totally depressed to the point of quitting Paxton Grange.

"As you know, Mum was too ill to attend the funeral today, but I am sure she will make a full recovery. However, this gives me a chance to make a confession to you, which I was unable to make to Dad."

Polly said nothing but the facial expression was enough for Angus to continue. "David Lampee and I are firm friends," stated Angus, "and that situation remains the same even though our fathers became arch enemies." It was Angus's wish that the friendship remained intact so what he was about to tell his sister must remain their secret. Taking this as guaranteed, he continued. "When we were looking for Archie's golf ball off the eighteenth fairway, and the time clock was running down, I remember that I had a couple of golf balls in my jacket pocket which I had nicked from Dad's store of balls which he kept in the house. He only played with the Titleist ball so I knew they were the same as the one he was using." "Stop, stop!" shouted Polly, lifting her hands momentarily over her ears and then lowering them again. Too late, Angus was in full flow now and with eyes welling tears he unloaded the truth. It wasn't the thought of losing the money that motivated him to make that insane decision; it was the thought of his father Archie losing the match due to a lost ball. He admitted to dropping a ball surreptitiously out of his jacket pocket and then walking away. Immediately regretting what he had done he retraced his steps back to the place where it lay, with the intention of putting it back in his pocket when the eagle-eyed Billy Smith spotted it, the rest was history.

Coughing and spluttering with tears streaming down his face, he proclaimed that Christian was wrong about Dad, Archie was no cheat, it was he, his son that caused the whole sorry episode. In his pocket he retrieved a golf ball and showed it his sister. He had picked it up after his dad had stormed off to the clubhouse. It was the only ball found at Paxton Grange golf course that had never been hit with a golf club.

Polly bereft, moved gingerly towards her brother, arms outstretched, and encompassed him in a sisterly embrace. "What a mess, what a bloody mess!"

Nobody

Chapter One

What a wonderful day it had been, the sun had shone all day long. There had been only two funerals that day and none of them had required my services, as they were both in a distant part of the cemetery. As afternoon passed to early evening I spotted a wake of buzzards overhead searching for a juicy rodent for their dinner. One of them may have been lucky as it dived towards an unkempt area of ground and disappeared behind a bush. Sometime later, and a first for me, a murmuration of starlings arrived swooping left and right through the dusky sky. This aerial ballet continued for a few minutes until the whole synchronized group decided to land simultaneously. How several hundred birds could fly in such close proximity to each other without colliding was totally beyond my comprehension, and will always remain a mystery to me. A few starlings had landed nearby which gave me a chance to make a closer examination. Despite perhaps appearing somewhat scruffy, they are in fact stunningly beautiful, with purple and green iridescence to their feathers, buff edges on the wing feathers, white speckles above and below, and a sharp yellow bill. Males and females are easy to tell apart; the base of the male's bill is pale blue while the female's is pale pink. They seemed to eat almost anything and everything until directed to leave by some unknown hand, at which they just took off and flew away.

After taking stock of the day's events I decided to settle down for the night and await the dawn with a new heightened expectancy. Little was I to know that before the sun rose I would be snatched from my resting place and heading for a new adventure.

Chapter Two

In the darkness I heard muffled voices and then spotted the pencil beam of what I thought was a torch heading my way. The light moved swiftly left then right until it focused on me. In the blink of an eye I was lifted up by an unseen hand and taken to the water tap and filled to the brim. Next followed a short staggered trek towards the voices of the torchbearers. Suddenly in the gloom I spotted an unfamiliar structure, which appeared to be a large tent erected around a grave. No sooner had I been deposited inside the tent when the sound of a small generator was heard, the noise of which was soft and low, it was then I noticed a diffused light filling the structure.

I was now able to take in the whole bizarre scene. The tent was not the type that normally springs to mind but a bespoke structure about seven feet tall with vertical ribbed walls for strength supporting a flat canvas roof that was perfectly square. The only door comprised a flimsy plastic sheet held closed by Velcro strips. The whole apparatus contained a number of people all dressed in thin plastic coverall suits that were white in colour. All eyes were fixed on the gravestone of Robert Strange, late of this parish.

"Right," said the man who brought me there, "my name is Ranek, I was at the funeral a year ago scanning for villains while paying my respects, hence my knowledge of the jug which you will need to top up the water-cooled generator." He pointed at four men leaning on spades.

"Introductions," he continued. "DCI Gallagher, overall officer in charge, Sally, forensic pathology, Julie, serious crime, Frank, parks and cemeteries, John, photographer. Old Bill, all four PCs gravedigging, driving and refreshments." Every name raised a finger in acknowledgement. "We have five hours to complete the job and return everything back to normal and be gone," Ranek said earnestly. "Let's give the lads some room and the rest of us retire to the transit van for a briefing. Let me know when you reach the coffin," he concluded.

It took over an hour of back-breaking work for the young constables to dig down and expose the coffin. A further thirty minutes passed unloading the support vehicle of ropes, planks, an A-frame, two lengths of firefighter hose, and some breaking-in tools. Finally, a much-deserved cuppa was had from a large flask. One of the team then walked over to the transit van and tapped on the side. No words were spoken. Within minutes the full team were back in the tent. Frank was the first to speak. "Good job so far, lads, it will be a lot easier to put the earth back, I assure you." Gallagher grimaced as he eyed the pile of earth. "Major miscalculation on my part," he exclaimed. "I didn't realize just how much room the earth would take up, we haven't got the coffin out yet, and it's bloody clay. The drinks are on me when we get back, and I mean drinks!"

Ranek took over. "OK, lads, set up the A-frame and bring the planks, hose and lines into play. Let's hope the practice drills were worth it. You have got thirty minutes." The men set to the task with aching backs.

Chapter Three

DCI Gallagher gently ushered Julie to one side and spoke to the Serious Crime Officer. "Let's go through Strange's history one more time and convince me that we are not on a wild goose chase here, and that I will not have my backside seriously kicked by him upstairs, and my reputation trashed." Julie dutifully began to recite the saga of Robert Strange and his criminal career and untimely death, while at the same time beckoning Sally from forensics to join them. She told of a daring robbery in 2010 where a large haul of cash and gems were stolen from a country house. Some seriously good detective work led to the arrest and conviction of Strange in which he received a sentence of eight years in prison. After some lengthy discussions with our villain, £100,000 was recovered from a hiding place and his sentence was duly halved. He became a free man in 2014. Julie explained that most of the gems were never found and Strange's explanation was that an accomplice took them as part of an agreement he had forged. Even under intense pressure with more prison time offered as an inducement, he refused to give up the person's name.

Later that year he went to Spain with his long-term girlfriend, Jose Banks, a very bright kid with a string of A levels to her name and a love of cars with outlandish colour schemes. It seems that they toured Europe for a few months and then Jose returned alone to the UK towards the end of the year. "This is where it started to get interesting," said Julie. She continued to lay out the bare bones of the story to the pair present who listened intently as if it was the first time they had been told the story. It appeared that Robert Strange took a trip to Sudan for reasons unknown, and he then subsequently contracted a deadly contagious parasitic disease to which he succumbed. The contact name on the passport was Jose, who arranged for the body of Strange to be flown back to the UK in a sealed coffin complete with a death certificate signed by a certain Doctor Mistori Burwelli. He was then buried here in the spring of 2015 and to all intents and purposes that was the end of the matter. Julie then went on to speak of an event which happened in the following year which gave rise to a potential clue that something spooky was going on.

Chapter Four

Julie went on to detail a number of events which, individually, were not sufficient enough to cause concern, but taken as a whole they were, in her opinion, a game changer that necessitated an exhumation of his grave to prove one way or the other that Strange was indeed dead.

It all started back in 2016 when the home of a Saudi prince was turned over and a large quantity of expensive jewellery was stolen. The Malaga police chief confirmed that the sophisticated alarm system had been bypassed and he was convinced that only one man was involved in the robbery as the sketchy CCTV confirmed. The villain was covered from head to foot in a coverall suit, which included his feet. He also wore gloves, which provided the first clue, as in the course of rotating the safe tumbles he found it helpful to partially remove his right glove leaving behind a partial print on the mechanism. Further analysis of the print was not conclusive, but a painstaking process at the headquarters of Europol's scientific division led to the names of four possible suspects being released. "As you know DNA is my speciality," Sally said, "but I can confirm that the probability factor given the tiny piece of evidence can only be put at between 50 and 65 per cent. Not much, I agree but a good basis for further investigation."

Julie thanked Sally for her contribution with the brief, stating that she put together a small team to find the four "possibles" and the likelihood of their involvement. Two were eliminated swiftly, one was a forger and the other an Internet scammer, and both considered totally the wrong profile for this job. The third suspect was a French man who was languishing in an Italian jail at the time of the robbery, which left Robert Strange, who we know was deceased. The trail had come to an end, she declared. It was her 'copper's nose' that led Julie to continue to make one final thrust in the case before she put it to bed and leave the matter with the Spanish police. Contact was made with the Sudanese Embassy and an interview requested with the help of an interpreter with a certain Doctor Mistori Burwelli to establish the circumstances of Strange's death.

A couple of days had passed when she received a call from the attaché at the embassy stating that an interview with the doctor could not be arranged in a professional capacity as Mistori Burwelli had been struck off by their medical council for corrupt practice, bribery and the falsification of documents. "Game back on," she stated with a broad smile. "I needed more evidence and wanted more time to forage." Pointing at Gallagher, she acknowledged that he had granted her two weeks to come up with something more substantial before he went to the top floor to set exhumation procedures in process.

Julie next visited the graveyard and asked questions of the staff, in particular whether a bright canary yellow Fiat Abarth had been seen parked near the grave. This vehicle was owned by Jose Banks, and the maintenance gang at the cemetery had no recollection of such a car. "Personally, this was the strongest indicator to me, as a woman, that this did not make any sense."

"Look," she continued eagerly, "we have one, a long-term love affair; two, numerous holidays together; three, regular visits when he was in prison, and yet she never comes to his grave after the funeral. I don't buy it, something isn't right, it stinks."

Julie then described how after much persuasion she was allowed to look at the phone records of Banks which yielded little out of the ordinary, just calls to local numbers and nothing suspicious. It was the text messages covertly obtained that yielded the big clues. Cryptic messages to an untraceable number in central Europe. These messages were never replied to until she received this bizarre text on her mobile: YES, FRIDAY! CRAP RUG LIST.

I now had time to recover from the ungainly move from my residence to the tent and was able to reflect on the burial of Robert Strange. It was a while ago but I was stuck by how few mourners were at the graveside, but having over heard a conversation stating that Strange had no siblings, and both his mother and father had passed on, this was not surprising. Only Jose Banks, dressed all in black and looking stunningly beautiful was there, along with her immediate family. My night-dreaming was suddenly broken when Julie continued to speak. "I can't take any credit for solving the puzzle of the text," she said, "but after toiling for a couple of days and getting nowhere I passed it to Joe in the office, a regular crossword puzzler of repute." She went on to say that Joe said the little x was a term of endearment which was pretty obvious but the rest of the message was a part anagram, Friday pointed to the day of the week and the rest of the words when unravelled could only spell 'plastic surgery': FRIDAY, PLASTIC SURGERY! "We now had, according to the subtext information from the mobile, a day and date of an operation," she said excitedly.

Julie was suddenly interrupted by one of the digging team who said they were ready to lift the coffin. The A-frame was in place above the hole, and planks were strategically placed to support the sides of the trench.

A length of strong plastic fire hose had been carefully threaded under each end of the coffin. "Haul away," commanded Gallagher, and the men, working as a team, brought the casket hand over hand to the surface. With military precision, the wooden box was swung through 90 degrees until it comfortably breached the trench. Finally the A-frame was temporarily removed and the coffin placed on a makeshift trestle made from planks lashed together with stout ropes.

It was now the turn of Sally to take the lead, which she did with precise, snappy commands. All present were told to don facemasks as a precautionary measure and a pair of the exhausted 'bobbies' were told to break the seal on the coffin and then step back. John the photographer was ordered to take photographs of the outside and then the inside of the sealed tomb when opened. Her primary role, Sally explained, was to take a DNA sample from the head of the corpse in the form of hair and establish a match, or not, back at the lab. "We have a reliable sample taken from Strange when he was first nicked and this should solve the mystery one way or another." One of the other pair of constables who were now resting approached Gallagher. "It was bloody heavy, boss, there is definitely something inside," was the pronouncement. Gallagher's face whitened at the news but he said nothing.

There was a crack, just like a rifle firing, and the lid moved a fraction, some unpleasant air escaped from within and Sally opened the coffin fully and gazed inside. All the rest of the team were pressed back to the walls of the tent as if the contents of the casket were about to spring out and grab them. A full twenty seconds passed before Sally spoke and then with the timing of a comedian delivering the punchline to a funny joke she uttered. "Can anyone remember that old tune that was sung by Louis Armstrong called 'I Ain't Got Nobody'? Well, that's exactly what we have got here, *no bloody body!*"

One at a time the group edged forward to peer inside. Looking back at them was part of a medium tree trunk cut to the size of an average man with two leather straps attaching it firmly to the base of the coffin. A smiley face had been cut out of the back at one end. Ranek was the first to speak. "He's alive, Strange is alive," he blurted. An ashen-faced Gallagher was next to contribute. "Put the coffin in the transit van," he ordered. "Make up all the equipment and restore the ground." Turning to Frank from cemeteries, he politely requested that he make the area look as though they had never been there and then, scratching his head, he left the tent. "It looks as though I am buying the drinks," smiled Ranek through clenched teeth and then, as an afterthought, he picked me up and stumbled back to my resting place.

Chapter Five

Almost a year had passed, when I recognized the familiar face of Julie near the tap, who was flanked by two other people who I didn't compute. It transpired that they were employed by a Sunday newspaper and were involved in a piece for the colour supplement magazine of the paper. She pointed to the grave in question and asserted that the name on the new headstone referred to the current occupant of the plot, and the original gravestone of Mr Strange had been removed. Unfortunately, the sorry saga of the grave's past history had been leaked to the press. The family of the deceased had been approached by the media with the angle of "using a second-hand grave" as the storyline. These approaches had led to great anguish to the family concerned who implored that they be left alone to grieve. The interview was agreed providing that lawyers from both the newspaper and the police authority agreed on what could be safely released before going to print.

While the photographer snapped away Julie gave a follow-on account of events since the exhumation. A tail and phone tap had been placed on Jose Banks because a reunion between her and Robert Strange seemed imminent. Sure enough, this proved to be the case as they met in Madrid within a week of the famous text. They were duly detained by the Spanish police, which was fortuitous as Strange had had a nose job in which its length had been shortened and the width marginally widened. The overall effect was to change the appearance of the face, some would say for the better. When interviewed he insisted that the injury to his nose had happened when he fell while climbing in the surrounding hills. Julie then went on to say that she and Ranek had spent a week in Spain to ascertain their position regarding the pair and to interview them about the fake death. His attitude was not helpful as he insisted on speaking only in Spanish with Jose acting as translator, and whom he subsequently married when paroled and quarantined within the city of Malaga. ("It's a tough life," I heard her scoff.) With reference to the fake death and the pending extradition request she continued that Strange was looking to start a new life with Jose and this was the only way to keep out of the spotlight because of his notoriety. "The man has a cult-like following both here and in Spain and I am concerned that no real charges will be bought. The Spanish police think the partial print evidence won't hold up under cross-examination and will be considered unsafe to proceed." "Where does that leave you in terms of extradition?" asked the reporter, "and what happened to the gems?" "I understand," Julie continued, "that Strange is in negotiations with the insurers who paid for *his* body to be repatriated to England from Sudan, to be recompensed in full if they drop the fraud charges. With regard to the gems, unofficially we think they were traded for bitcoins and then reverted to cash. That leaves us with the fake death scenario. Who knows about the outcome? If you are desirous of an interview with the pair just pop over to Malaga and look for a couple in a shocking pink Mercedes sports, they answer to the title of Mr and Mrs Grasten since he changed his name." "Grasten," said the reporter quizzically. "Yes, Grasten," replied Julie. "I'm sure you can work it out!" Suddenly Julie's mobile warbled. "Excuse me, it's the boss, Mr Gallagher," she said. "Good God!" she blurted to the reporter. "Impeccable source, Robert Strange Grasten critically injured. Tyre shot out on mountain road by assassins on motorbike."

Lightning Source UK Ltd.
Milton Keynes UK
UKHW012045211021
392610UK00001B/59

9 781781 329740